TAKE ME OUT TO THE Ball Game

In Canada
Fitzhenry & Whiteside Limited
195 Allstate Parkway
Markham, Ontario L3R 4T8
www.fitzhenry.ca

In the United States
Fitzhenry & Whiteside Limited
121 Harvard Avenue, Suite 2
Allston, Massachusetts 02134
godwit@fitzhenry.ca

10 9 8 7 6 5 4 3 2 1

National Library of Canada Cataloguing in Publication

Kovalski, Maryann
Take me out to the ballgame / Maryann Kovalski.

For children aged 4-7.
ISBN 1-55041-897-1 (bound)—ISBN 1-55041-899-8 (pbk.)

I. Title.

PS8571.O96T34 2004   jC813'.54   C2004-900158-2

U.S. Publisher Cataloging-in-Publication Data
(Library of Congress Standards)

Kovalski, Maryann.
Take me out to the ballgame / Maryann Kovalski. —1st ed.
[32] p. : col. ill. ; cm.
Summary Jenny and Joanna love their imaginative and exciting grandmother.
One day grandmother arrives to take them on an outing, even if it is a school day.
ISBN 1-55041-897-1
ISBN 1-55041-899-8   (pbk.)
1. Baseball — Fiction. 2. Grandmothers — Fiction. I. Title.
[E] 21   PZ7.K 683Ta 2004

Fitzhenry & Whiteside acknowledges with thanks the Canada Council for the Arts,
the Government of Canada through its Book Publishing Industry Development Program,
and the Ontario Arts Council for their support of our publishing program.

Printed in Hong Kong
Design by Wycliffe Smith Design Inc.

M A R Y A N N   K O V A L S K I

TAKE ME OUT TO THE

Ball Game

Fitzhenry & Whiteside

Jenny and Joanna were dressing for school when the doorbell rang. It was Grandma! She whispered something to Mama and Papa.

"But they can't go today," said Mama. "Today is a school day."

"Sometimes, some things are more important than school," said Grandma.

Papa agreed.

"Well, just this once," said Mama.

What could be more important than school? Joanna wondered.

Jenny and Joanna ran into Grandma's arms.

"What could be more important than school?" begged Jenny.

Grandma wouldn't tell them. She just smiled and said, "Hurry. We have things to do before you find out."

At school, Grandma whispered to the principal. He smiled and said, "Well, just this once." Jenny and Joanna begged Grandma to tell but she wouldn't. She only smiled.

She only smiled all through breakfast.

She only smiled all the way to the subway.

She wouldn't tell them while they rode the train.

It was Jenny who saw it first. Then Joanna saw it too.

But it was Grandma who sang out loud.

♪ 'Take me out to the ballgame. ♪

Buy me some♪

♪ peanuts and Cracker ♪ Jacks.

For it's...One !

Two!

Three strikes
You're out!

"You were right, Grandma," said Joanna.
"Baseball is more important than school!"
Jenny agreed.
"Well…just this once," said Grandma.

Take Me Out to the Ballgame

Words by Jack Norworth   Music by Albert von Tilzer

Take me out to the ball game.

Take me out with the crowd._____

Buy me some pea-nuts and Crack - er Jacks.

I don't care if I nev - er get back! For it's

root, root, root for the home team. If

they don't win it's a shame._____ For it's...

One! Two! Three strikes, you're out! At the

old... ball... game. _____